THE WONDERFUL WIZARD OF OZ

Library of Congress Cataloging-in-Publication Data

Mabie, Grace, (date)
    The wonderful Wizard of Oz / by L. Frank Baum; retold by Grace
Mabie; illustrated by Tom Newsom.
      p.   cm. (Troll illustrated classics)
    Summary: After a cyclone transports her to the land of Oz, Dorothy
must seek out the great Wizard in order to return to Kansas.
    ISBN 0-8167-2864-X (lib. bdg.)   ISBN 0-8167-2865-8 (pbk.)
    [1. Fantasy.] I. Newsom, Tom, ill. II. Baum, L. Frank (Lyman
Frank), 1856-1919. Wizard of Oz. III. Title.
PZ7.M1118Wo 1993
[Fic]—dc20   92-12704

Printed in the United States of America.
10 9 8 7 6 5 4 3 2

THE WONDERFUL WIZARD OF OZ

L. FRANK BAUM

Retold by
Grace Mabie

Illustrated by
Tom Newsom

Troll Associates

Dorothy lived in the middle of the great Kansas prairie, with Uncle Henry, who was a farmer, and Aunt Em, who was the farmer's wife. They lived in a little gray house. Not only the house was gray. Everything in that flat land, as far as the eye could see, was dull and without joy.

Only Dorothy was not gray and grim—Dorothy and her little black dog, Toto. Toto played all day long. Dorothy played with him, and loved him dearly.

Today, however, they were not playing. Dorothy stood in the doorway with Toto in her arms. Her Uncle Henry sat on the doorstep. They looked out and saw the grass waving under the dark sky. The wind began to wail as a storm approached.

Suddenly Uncle Henry stood up. "There's a cyclone coming, Em," he called into the house. "I'm going to take care of the horses."

Aunt Em came to the door. "Quick, Dorothy!" she screamed. "Run for the cellar!" Then she turned and ran back inside. She flung open a trap door and hurried into the cyclone cellar beneath the house.

As Dorothy ran for safety, Toto jumped out of her arms. Dorothy tried to get her little dog out from under the bed, where he was hiding. Just then, there was a great shriek of wind. The house shook so much that Dorothy's feet slipped out from under her, and she sat down hard on the floor.

Then a strange thing happened.

The house whirled around—and began to rise into the air! It was dark, and the wind howled. The house was in the center of a great, whirling cyclone!

Toto did not like this at all. He ran around the room, barking loudly, until Dorothy caught him. They sat together on the floor as hour after hour passed, and the house continued to ride the cyclone.

Dorothy grew very tired. At last she crawled over the swaying floor to her bed, and lay down with Toto beside her. Soon they were both fast asleep.

Dorothy was awakened by a tremendous thud. The house had landed at last! The room was filled with sunshine. Dorothy sprang to her feet and ran outside to see where she was.

The little girl could hardly believe her eyes. She was in a world of marvelous beauty. Green grass was all around her, and banks of gorgeous flowers were everywhere. Beautiful birds sang in the trees. It was all so colorful!

While Dorothy stood looking eagerly at these sights, she saw a group of strange people coming toward her. Three of them were men, all dressed in blue. With them was a little old woman.

"Welcome to the land of the Munchkins, noble sorceress," the woman said when the group reached Dorothy. "Thank you for killing the Wicked Witch of the East. Now the Munchkins are free!"

"I'm not a sorceress. I'm Dorothy," the girl explained. She was very puzzled by all that was happening. "And I didn't kill anything."

"Your house did," replied the little old woman, laughing. "It fell on top of the Wicked Witch, and she is quite dead." She pointed to two feet sticking out from under the corner of the house. The feet wore beautiful silver shoes.

"Oh dear!" cried Dorothy. "What shall I do?"

"There is nothing to be done," said the woman. "The Wicked Witch made the Munchkins work day and night. They are very grateful to you for giving them back their freedom."

"Are you a Munchkin?" Dorothy asked.

"No, but I am their friend. I am the Witch of the North, and I am a good witch. The Witch of the South is also a good witch. But there is one more witch, the Wicked Witch of the West. And she is very wicked indeed."

Just then the Munchkins gave a loud shout and pointed to where the dead witch lay. Her feet had disappeared, and only the silver shoes remained.

"She was so old," explained the Witch of the North, "that she dried up quickly in the sun. Now the silver shoes are yours to keep," she told Dorothy. She picked up the shoes and handed them to the little girl.

"Thank you," Dorothy said. "But I want to go home to Kansas. Can you help me find my way back?"

Everyone looked confused. No one had ever heard of Kansas. Dorothy began to cry. The Munchkins were so soft-hearted that they began to cry, too. As for the little old woman, she took off her cap, balanced it on her nose, and counted to three. On the cap, these words suddenly appeared:

LET DOROTHY GO TO THE CITY OF EMERALDS.

"Where is the City of Emeralds?" Dorothy asked. "And how can I get back to Kansas?"

"The City of Emeralds is in the center of our country, the Land of Oz," the old woman explained. "The great Wizard of Oz lives there. Perhaps he can tell you how to get back to Kansas."

"How do I get there?" asked Dorothy.

"The road to the City of Emeralds is paved with yellow brick," said the Witch. She gave Dorothy a special kiss on the forehead. "My kiss will keep you safe on your journey, for no one would dare injure a person who has been kissed by the Witch of the North." Then the kindly old Witch twirled around three times and disappeared.

Dorothy put on the silver shoes and filled her basket with bread from the farmhouse. Then she and Toto started out for the Emerald City, following the yellow brick road.

Dorothy passed many blue houses as she walked, for blue was the Munchkins' favorite color. After going many miles, she stopped to rest near a corn field. A Scarecrow stuffed with straw was stuck on a pole in the field, to keep the birds away from the corn.

While Dorothy was looking at the Scarecrow's painted face, she was surprised to see one of the eyes slowly wink at her. None of the scarecrows in Kansas ever winked!

"Good day," said the Scarecrow in a husky voice.

"Did you say something?" asked the little girl.

"Certainly. How do you do?"

"I'm pretty well, thank you," Dorothy replied politely. "How are you?"

"I'm not feeling well," the Scarecrow told her. "I'm tired of being perched up here day and night. Will you help me get down?"

Dorothy reached up and lifted the straw man off the pole. He was very light. "Thank you," he said when she had set him down on the ground. "I feel like a new man." Then he asked Dorothy where she was going.

"To the Emerald City, to see the great Wizard," said Dorothy. She told him of all the amazing things that had happened and how the Wizard was her only hope of getting back to Kansas.

"Where is the Emerald City?" asked the Scarecrow. "And who is the Wizard?"

"Why, don't you know?" Dorothy asked in surprise.

"No. I don't know anything. You see, I am stuffed, so I have no brains at all," the Scarecrow answered sadly. "Do you think the Wizard of Oz will give me some brains?"

"I don't know," Dorothy replied. "But you may come with us. We'll ask Oz to do all he can for you."

"Thank you," said the Scarecrow. And together they set off down the road.

They spent the night in a cottage near the woods. In the morning, they were awakened by a deep groaning noise. Dorothy walked into the forest and heard the noise again. Then she saw something shining between the trees, and ran to see what it was.

There was a man there, made entirely out of tin. He stood perfectly motionless.

"What can I do for you?" Dorothy asked.

"Get an oilcan from the cottage and oil my joints," answered the Tin Woodman. "They're all rusted. I've been this way for over a year."

Dorothy oiled his neck first, and then his arms and legs. Soon the Tin Woodman could move freely. He thanked her again and again. "You have saved my life," he said. "How did you happen to be here?"

Dorothy told him of their trip to see the great Wizard. The Tin Woodman looked very thoughtful.

"Do you think Oz would give me a heart?" he asked. "I have wanted one for a long time."

"I don't know," answered Dorothy. "But you can come along and ask him."

The three companions and Toto went on down the yellow brick road. The woods grew dark and thick around them, and it got harder and harder to walk.

Suddenly a great Lion bounded into the road with a terrible roar. He struck the Scarecrow with one huge paw and sent him spinning. Then he scratched the Tin Woodman with his sharp claws. Little Toto ran up to the Lion and barked. The terrible beast opened his mouth wide to bite him.

Dorothy was afraid Toto would be killed. Without thinking of the danger, she ran up to the Lion and slapped him on the nose. "Don't you dare bite Toto, you big coward!" Dorothy yelled. "You ought to be ashamed of yourself, picking on something so much smaller than you!"

At this, the Lion started to sob. "You're right. I am a coward. Only a coward would try to bite such a little thing." He wiped his eyes with the tip of his tail. "I have been a coward since the day I was born."

"But the King of Beasts should not be a coward," said the Scarecrow.

"I know, but I can't help it," cried the Lion. "Whenever I roar, my heart beats very fast."

"At least you have a heart," said the Tin Woodman.

"And a brain," sighed the Scarecrow.

"But I have no courage!" wailed the Lion, wringing out his tail.

"I know," said Dorothy. "You could come with us and ask the Wizard of Oz for some courage."

This pleased the Lion very much. The little group set off on their journey once more, with the Lion walking along at Dorothy's side.

The travelers camped out under a large tree that night, for there were no houses nearby. But the tree made a good, thick covering to protect them from the dew. And Dorothy built a splendid fire with the great pile of wood the Tin Woodman chopped for her, so they really were quite cozy.

They walked through the forest for another night and day. Soon the trees began to thin out. The travelers came to a broad river running through beautiful green meadows. The yellow brick road continued on the other side.

"How shall we cross the river?" asked Dorothy.

"That's easily done," replied the Scarecrow. "The Tin Woodman must build a raft so we can float to the other side."

So the Tin Woodman chopped down many small trees, bound them together, and built a fine raft. Everyone climbed aboard, and they set out over the water.

They got along quite well at first, but when they reached the middle of the river, the swift current swept the raft downstream. They floated farther and farther away from the yellow brick road.

"This is bad," said the Tin Woodman. "If we stray much farther, we'll be trespassing on the land of the Wicked Witch of the West. She will enchant us and make us her slaves."

"Something must be done to save us," said the Lion. He sprang into the water and motioned to the Tin Woodman to grab his tail. With powerful strokes, he pulled the raft safely to the other side.

Here the forest opened up into vast fields full of lovely
flowers. The ground was a colorful carpet of blossoms. As
the friends walked along, they smelled the spicy scent of
thousands of scarlet poppies.

Dorothy and her friends did not know that the powerful
smell of the poppies casts a magic spell. All that breathe
it fall fast asleep and, if not carried away from the flowers,
will sleep forever.

Presently, Dorothy's eyes grew heavy, and she fell into a deep sleep among the poppies. Even the strong Lion could not keep his eyes open. But since the Scarecrow and the Tin Woodman were not made of flesh, they were not troubled by the flowers' scent. It was up to them to rescue their sleeping friends.

Making a chair with their arms, the Scarecrow and the Tin Woodman carried Dorothy out of the field. They set her down near the river, where they waited for the fresh breeze to wake her. But they could not move the Lion, for he was much too big and heavy. Sadly, they left him to sleep on the sweet grass of the poppy field.

As they sat on the bank, the Scarecrow and the Tin Woodman saw a great yellow wildcat chasing a little field mouse. The Tin Woodman could not bear to think of the wildcat hurting such a pretty, helpless creature. He raised his axe, and as the wildcat ran by, he killed it.

"Oh, thank you!" said the mouse in a squeaky voice. "You have done a great deed, for I am a Queen—Queen of all the field mice!"

"It is a pleasure to meet you," said the Tin Woodman, bowing to her. As they talked, hundreds of field mice gathered around them.

"Is there anything we can do to repay you for saving the life of our Queen?" the mice asked.

"Oh yes," said the Scarecrow quickly. "You can save our friend, the Lion. He is fast asleep in the poppy field, and will surely die if we don't get him out."

The mice quickly agreed to help. The Tin Woodman set to work making a cart out of wood. Meanwhile, the Queen ordered all the mice to find lengths of string. Then the mice pulled the cart to where the Lion lay sleeping.

The Tin Woodman and the Scarecrow lifted the heavy animal onto the cart, and the mice pulled and pulled until the Lion was safely out of the poppy field.

"If ever you need us again," said the Queen to Dorothy, who was awake by now, "come out into the fields and call me." The Queen gave Dorothy a whistle as a token of their friendship. Then she waved good-bye and ran off through the grass.

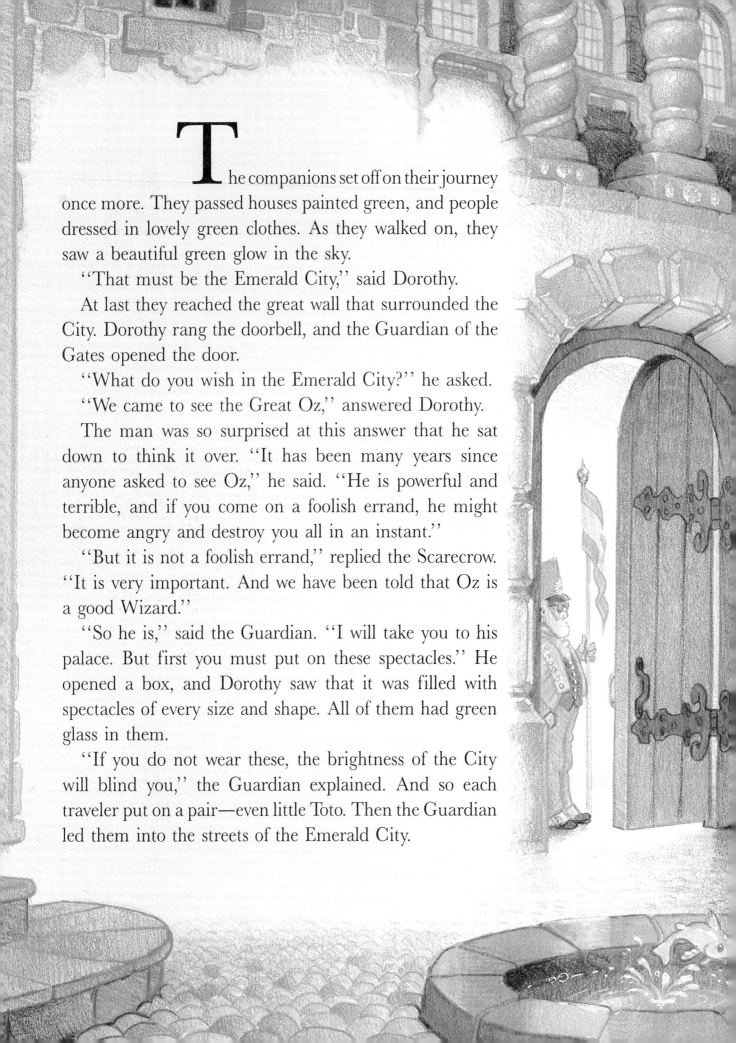

The companions set off on their journey once more. They passed houses painted green, and people dressed in lovely green clothes. As they walked on, they saw a beautiful green glow in the sky.

"That must be the Emerald City," said Dorothy.

At last they reached the great wall that surrounded the City. Dorothy rang the doorbell, and the Guardian of the Gates opened the door.

"What do you wish in the Emerald City?" he asked.

"We came to see the Great Oz," answered Dorothy.

The man was so surprised at this answer that he sat down to think it over. "It has been many years since anyone asked to see Oz," he said. "He is powerful and terrible, and if you come on a foolish errand, he might become angry and destroy you all in an instant."

"But it is not a foolish errand," replied the Scarecrow. "It is very important. And we have been told that Oz is a good Wizard."

"So he is," said the Guardian. "I will take you to his palace. But first you must put on these spectacles." He opened a box, and Dorothy saw that it was filled with spectacles of every size and shape. All of them had green glass in them.

"If you do not wear these, the brightness of the City will blind you," the Guardian explained. And so each traveler put on a pair—even little Toto. Then the Guardian led them into the streets of the Emerald City.

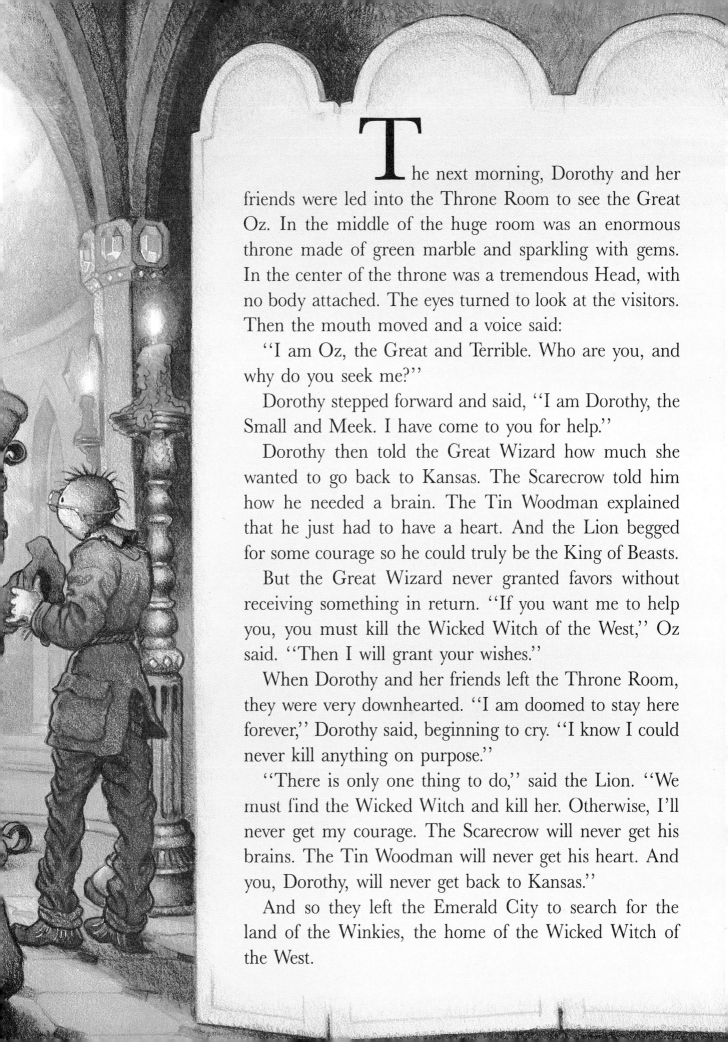

The next morning, Dorothy and her friends were led into the Throne Room to see the Great Oz. In the middle of the huge room was an enormous throne made of green marble and sparkling with gems. In the center of the throne was a tremendous Head, with no body attached. The eyes turned to look at the visitors. Then the mouth moved and a voice said:

"I am Oz, the Great and Terrible. Who are you, and why do you seek me?"

Dorothy stepped forward and said, "I am Dorothy, the Small and Meek. I have come to you for help."

Dorothy then told the Great Wizard how much she wanted to go back to Kansas. The Scarecrow told him how he needed a brain. The Tin Woodman explained that he just had to have a heart. And the Lion begged for some courage so he could truly be the King of Beasts.

But the Great Wizard never granted favors without receiving something in return. "If you want me to help you, you must kill the Wicked Witch of the West," Oz said. "Then I will grant your wishes."

When Dorothy and her friends left the Throne Room, they were very downhearted. "I am doomed to stay here forever," Dorothy said, beginning to cry. "I know I could never kill anything on purpose."

"There is only one thing to do," said the Lion. "We must find the Wicked Witch and kill her. Otherwise, I'll never get my courage. The Scarecrow will never get his brains. The Tin Woodman will never get his heart. And you, Dorothy, will never get back to Kansas."

And so they left the Emerald City to search for the land of the Winkies, the home of the Wicked Witch of the West.

The Wicked Witch was in her castle. She had only one eye, yet it was as powerful as a telescope and could see everywhere. When the Witch saw Dorothy and her friends on her land, she was very angry. She blew on a silver whistle hanging around her neck. A pack of ferocious wolves ran in and sat at her feet.

"Go to these people," the Witch ordered the wolves, "and tear them to pieces."

But when the Tin Woodman heard the wolves coming, he seized his axe and killed every one of them. This made the Witch even angrier. She sent a flock of crows to peck at them.

The wild crows flew in a great flock toward Dorothy
and her companions. Dorothy was frightened, but the
Scarecrow knew what to do with crows. Soon they, too,
all lay dead in a heap.

Now the Witch was angrier than ever. She sent a swarm
of black bees to sting them. But Dorothy and her friends
covered themselves with the Scarecrow's straw, so that the
bees saw only the Tin Woodman. When they tried to
sting his metal body, all their stingers broke. They fell
down dead like little heaps of coal.

The Wicked Witch was so angry, she stamped her feet and tore her hair. She could not understand how all her plans to destroy these strangers had failed. But she was a powerful Witch, as well as a wicked one, and she soon made up her mind what to do.

In her cupboard, the Witch had a Golden Cap. This cap had a charm. Whoever owned it could call three times upon the Winged Monkeys, who would obey any order they were given. The Witch put on her Golden Cap and said the magic words:

> "Ep-pe, pep-pe, kak-ke!
> Hil-lo, hol-lo, hel-lo!
> Ziz-zy, zuz-zy, zik!"

The sky grew dark, and a low rumble sounded through the air. There was the rushing of many wings, and the Winged Monkeys swooped down to do the Witch's bidding. She ordered them to destroy the visitors, except for the Lion. He looked big and strong, and the Witch wanted to make him her slave.

The Monkeys flew swiftly to where Dorothy and her friends were walking. They dropped the Tin Woodman over some rocks, and he fell to pieces. Then they scattered the Scarecrow's straw all over. But upon reaching Dorothy, they saw the kiss of the good Witch of the North on her. As long as she had this mark, they could not hurt her. So they carried Dorothy and the Lion back to the Witch's castle.

"We dare not harm this little girl," the leader of the Monkeys told the Witch. "She is protected by the Power of Good, and that is greater than the Power of Evil."

The Wicked Witch was surprised and worried when she saw the mark on Dorothy's forehead. She knew that she dared not hurt the girl in any way. Then she saw the silver shoes on Dorothy's feet, and she began to tremble. But she realized that Dorothy had no idea of the power the shoes held, and that thought gave her confidence.

She made Dorothy her slave, and forced the little girl to cook and clean and work very hard. As for the Lion, the Witch locked him in a cage. She thought she would harness him to her chariot like a horse. But every time the Witch went near him, the Lion roared so loudly that the Witch was afraid. She told him he would get no food until he did as she wished.

Dorothy found ways to feed the Cowardly Lion, but she was very sad. Sometimes she would cry for hours, thinking about her Aunt Em and Uncle Henry, and wondered if she would ever see her home again.

The Wicked Witch wanted nothing more than to own the silver shoes that Dorothy always wore. She tried to think of ways to trick Dorothy into taking them off. Finally she hit upon a plan. She put a bar of iron in the middle of the kitchen floor, then used her magic to make it invisible. When Dorothy walked across the room, she tripped over it and fell. She was not hurt—but one of the silver shoes fell off. Cackling at her good fortune, the Witch snatched it up.

"Give me back my shoe!" Dorothy demanded.

"I will not," replied the Witch.

"You are a wicked creature!" Dorothy cried. She was so angry that she picked up a bucket of water and dashed it over the Witch, soaking her from head to foot.

The wicked woman gave a loud cry. Then she began to shrink! "I'm melting!" screamed the Witch. "Oh, now see what you have done!"

"Oh, I'm so sorry!" Dorothy said. She was truly frightened to see the Witch melting away. Soon there was nothing left of her but a shapeless mass spreading over the kitchen floor.

Dorothy put on the silver shoe once more. Then she ran outside to free the Lion and tell him they were no longer prisoners.

Dorothy and the Lion were free, but they missed the Scarecrow and the Tin Woodman. They went out and found them where the Winged Monkeys had left them. The Winkies, who were now free from the Witch's slavery, worked day and night to make the Scarecrow and the Tin Woodman as good as new.

The little group was overjoyed to be together again. They decided to go back to the Great Wizard, who had promised to grant all their wishes if they killed the Wicked Witch. Before they left, Dorothy went to the cupboard to pack some food for the journey. There she found the Golden Cap. She thought it was quite pretty, so she put it on.

The travelers started off due east, toward the rising sun. But at noon the sun was directly overhead, and soon they were lost.

"I haven't the courage to keep walking all day without getting anywhere," said the Lion.

Dorothy sat down on the grass. "Suppose we call the field mice," she suggested. "They could probably tell us the way to the Emerald City." She blew the little whistle the Queen of the Mice had given to her. In a few minutes, they heard the pattering of many tiny feet.

"What can I do for my friends?" asked the Queen of the Mice.

"We have lost our way," Dorothy said. "How can we get to the Emerald City?"

"I could tell you how to get there, but it is a long way off," said the Queen. Then she noticed the Golden Cap on Dorothy's head. "Why don't you use the charm of the Cap to call the Winged Monkeys?" she asked. "They will carry you to the Emerald City in less than an hour."

"I didn't know the Cap had a charm," Dorothy said in surprise. She took off the cap and recited the words written in the lining:

"Ep-pe, pep-pe, kak-ke!
Hil-lo, hol-lo, hel-lo!
Ziz-zy, zuz-zy, zik!"

With a great flapping of wings and much chattering, the Winged Monkeys swooped down before them. "What is your command?" asked their leader.

Dorothy no sooner told them to take them to the Emerald City, than the Monkeys picked each of them up and flew away. The Scarecrow and the Tin Woodman were frightened at first, for they remembered how badly the Monkeys had treated them before. But they soon saw that the Monkeys meant them no harm. Then they rode through the air quite cheerfully, and had a fine time looking down at the pretty gardens and woods far below.

Soon the shining green walls of the Emerald City rose before them. The Monkeys set the travelers down carefully before the gate, then quickly flew away.

Dorothy rang the bell several times. Finally the door was opened by the Guardian who had met them the first time.

"What! Are you back again?" he exclaimed in surprise. "How did the Wicked Witch ever let you go?"

"She could not help it," said the Scarecrow. "Dorothy melted her."

The Guardian of the Gate bowed deeply before Dorothy. Then he took them in and gave them green glasses to protect their eyes, just as he had done before.

Dorothy and her friends thought the Great Wizard would send for them at once, but he did not. Many days passed without a word from him. Finally, the Scarecrow sent a message to Oz. He said that if the Wizard did not let them in to see him right away, they would call the Winged Monkeys to help them. When Oz heard that, he was so frightened that he sent word for Dorothy and the others to come to the Throne Room first thing the next morning.

When they entered the Throne Room, they did not see the great Head of the Wizard as they had before. Instead, the room was empty.

Presently, they heard a Voice speaking out of the emptiness. "I am Oz, the Great and Terrible," it said. "Why do you seek me?"

"We have come to claim our promises," Dorothy said.

"What promises?"

"You promised to send me back to Kansas if I killed the Wicked Witch of the West. I melted her, and she is dead," Dorothy explained.

"And you promised to give me brains," said the Scarecrow.

"And you promised to give me a heart," said the Tin Woodman.

"And you promised to give me courage," said the Cowardly Lion.

"I must have time to think it over," said the Voice.

"You've had plenty of time already," said the Tin Woodman angrily.

"We won't wait a day longer," said the Scarecrow.

The Lion gave a loud roar that startled everyone, especially poor little Toto. The dog jumped back and knocked over a screen standing in the corner. As it fell with a crash, they all saw a little old man standing behind it. He looked very startled.

"Who are you?" the Tin Woodman shouted.

"I am Oz...the Great...and Terrible...." the man said in a trembling voice.

"But I thought Oz was a great Head," said Dorothy.

"I was just making believe," said the man meekly. "The Head was just a trick." He took them to a chamber where he kept the great Head. It was just thick paper with a fierce, painted-on face. "I hung it from the ceiling with wire," the man explained. "Please don't tell anyone the truth about me. Everyone here thinks I am a great Wizard. I'll be in terrible trouble if I'm found out."

"You ought to be ashamed of yourself for being such a humbug," the Scarecrow said.

"I am. But it was the only thing I could do. Sit down, and I will tell you my story."

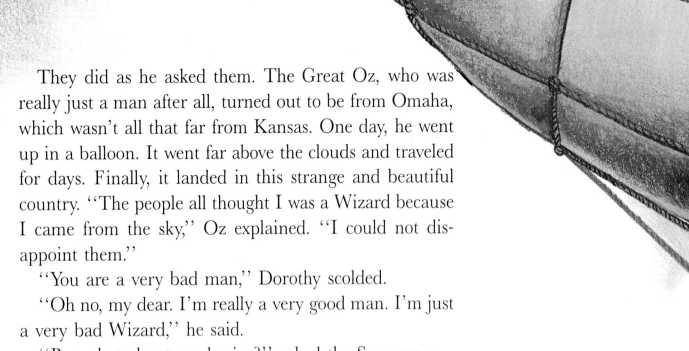

They did as he asked them. The Great Oz, who was really just a man after all, turned out to be from Omaha, which wasn't all that far from Kansas. One day, he went up in a balloon. It went far above the clouds and traveled for days. Finally, it landed in this strange and beautiful country. "The people all thought I was a Wizard because I came from the sky," Oz explained. "I could not disappoint them."

"You are a very bad man," Dorothy scolded.

"Oh no, my dear. I'm really a very good man. I'm just a very bad Wizard," he said.

"But what about my brains?" asked the Scarecrow.

"And my heart?" asked the Tin Woodman.

"And my courage?" asked the Lion.

"You don't need them," the Wizard said. "You've had them all along." But they looked as though they didn't believe him, so the Wizard said, "Come back tomorrow morning and I will see what I can do."

"But how am I to get back to Kansas?" Dorothy asked.

"I will think of something," the Wizard promised.

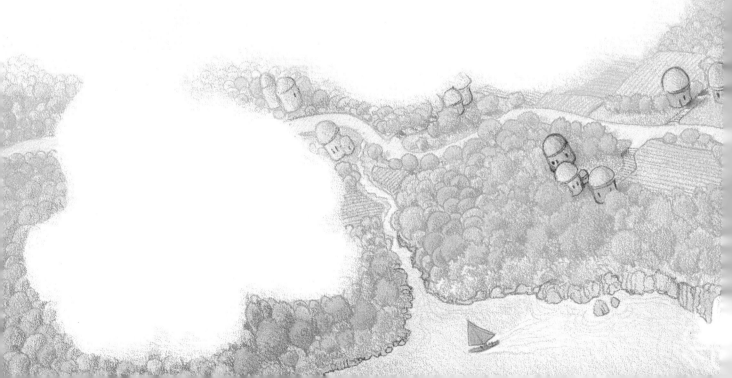

The next morning, the Scarecrow was the first one to see the Wizard.

"You must excuse me for taking your head off," said Oz, "but I have to do it to put your brains in their proper place."

"That's all right," said the Scarecrow, "as long as it will be a better head when you put it on again."

Then Oz stuffed the Scarecrow's head with a mixture of bran and pins and needles. This was so the Scarecrow would have bran-new brains and be very sharp-witted.

The Tin Woodman went next to get his heart.

"I'm sorry I have to cut a hole in your chest," said Oz, "but how else can I give you a heart?"

"Don't worry," said the Tin Woodman. "I won't even feel it."

Oz cut through the tin. Inside the Woodman's chest he placed a beautiful silk heart stuffed with sawdust. Then he patched up the hole he had made.

"Now you have a heart anyone would be proud of," said Oz.

"Thank you," said the Tin Woodman, grinning as wide as his metal jaw would go. He hurried away to show his friends.

Next the Cowardly Lion went to the Throne Room to get his dose of courage. Oz went to the cupboard, got out a little green bottle, and poured its contents into a bowl.

"What is that?" asked the Lion.

"If it were inside of you, it would be courage," the Wizard told him. "Drink up."

The Lion drank every drop.

"How do you feel?" asked Oz.

"Full of courage," roared the Lion. He went joyfully back to tell his friends the good news.

Oz smiled to himself at his success in giving the Scarecrow, the Tin Woodman, and the Lion exactly what they wanted. "How can I help being a humbug, when all these people make me do impossible things? It was easy to make the Scarecrow and the Lion and the Woodman happy, because they imagined I could do it. But it will take more than imagination to carry Dorothy back to Kansas. Still, I think I know of a way it can be done."

When Dorothy went to see the Wizard, Oz was deep in thought. "You got here in a cyclone," he said at last, "and I got here in a balloon. We both came through the air. I can't make a cyclone, but I believe I can build a balloon. If you help me sew the silk together, we can soon be on our way."

"We!" exclaimed Dorothy. "Are you going with me?"

"Yes, of course," replied Oz. "I'm tired of being a humbug and being shut up in this castle all day."

For the next three days, Dorothy and the Wizard were very busy. They cut strips of green silk and sewed them together, until they had a bag more than twenty feet long. Then Oz painted it on the inside with a coat of glue to make it airtight. Finally, they attached a clothes basket to the balloon, and they were ready to go.

Oz called his people together and announced that he was going to visit another Wizard who lived in the clouds. "While I am gone, the Scarecrow will rule over you," Oz instructed.

While everyone stared in curiosity, the Tin Woodman lit a huge fire to warm the air in the silken bag. Slowly, the balloon swelled and rose into the air.

Oz got into the basket as it strained against the ropes holding it to the ground. "Come on, Dorothy!" he called. "Hurry up, or the balloon will fly away!"

But Dorothy had gone after Toto, who was chasing a kitten in the crowd. At last she found him. Scooping the little dog up in her arms, she ran back toward the balloon. She was within a few steps of it when the balloon broke free of its ropes with a loud *crack*!

"Come back!" Dorothy screamed as the balloon rose swiftly in the air without her.

"I can't, my dear," Oz called back. "Good-bye!"

"Good-bye!" shouted everyone, as all eyes turned upward to watch the Wizard rising farther and farther into the sky. That was the last anyone ever saw of him.

Dorothy wept bitterly at the loss of her only chance to get home to Kansas. The Scarecrow was sorry to see Dorothy so upset. He thought so hard that the pins and needles began to stick out of his new brains. Finally he said, "Why not call the Winged Monkeys? Perhaps they can carry you through the sky back to Kansas."

Everyone said this was a splendid idea. So Dorothy got out the Golden Cap and called the Winged Monkeys. But their leader shook his head sadly when he heard Dorothy's request.

"That cannot be done," he said. "We belong to this country and cannot leave it." And they flew off.

The Scarecrow thought some more. He called the Guardian of the Gates and asked for his advice.

"Why don't you ask Glinda, the Witch of the South?" the Guardian suggested. "She is the most powerful of all the Witches. She rules over the Quadlings, and is very good to them. Just take the road to the south, and you will find her."

Dorothy and her friends began their journey the next morning. It was good to be out in the country again. The Lion sniffed the fresh air with delight, while Toto ran around them, barking merrily and chasing moths and butterflies. Even Dorothy was cheerful, for she was once more filled with the hope of getting home.

On the second day of their trip, they came to a forest so thick, they could not get by. At last, the Scarecrow found a place to enter. But as he walked under the branches, they bent down, twisted around him, and flung him away.

Of course, this did not hurt the Scarecrow, but it surprised him very much. The Tin Woodman raised his axe as if he were going to cut the trees down. This scared the trees so much, they let the group pass.

At the other end of the forest, they came to a smooth, high wall, which seemed to be made of china. There was no way to climb it, so the Tin Woodman made a ladder out of wood from the forest. In this way, they were all able to get to the top of the wall. What they saw there filled them with amazement.

Before them was a great stretch of country made entirely of china. The people and animals and houses were all made of porcelain, too, and were quite small and delicate.

Dorothy and her friends climbed down the wall and began to cross this strange country. Nearby, they saw a milkmaid milking a cow. Toto started to bark, and the cow gave a great kick. It knocked over the stool and the pail with a great clatter.

"See what you've done!" cried the milkmaid angrily. "My cow has broken her leg right off. Now I must have it glued on again, and she'll never be the same."

"I'm very sorry," Dorothy said. "Please forgive us."

"We must be very careful here," said the kind-hearted Tin Woodman. "We don't want to hurt any of these people."

As they walked along, they met a lovely china Princess. She and Dorothy began to talk. "You are so beautiful," Dorothy said. "Won't you let me carry you back to Kansas?"

"That would make me very unhappy," said the Princess. "Here in our own country, we can talk and move around as we please. But whenever any of us are taken away, our joints stiffen. We can only stand straight and look pretty, and that is not pleasant at all."

"I would not make you unhappy for all the world!" exclaimed Dorothy. And so they said good-bye to the china Princess, and continued on their journey.

After about an hour, the travelers came to the other side of the china country and found another china wall. But this one was lower than the first, and by standing on the Lion's back, they were able to get over it easily.

Soon Dorothy and her companions came to a steep hill, covered from top to bottom with huge pieces of rock. "That will be a hard climb," said the Scarecrow, "but we must get over the hill."

They had almost reached the first rock when they heard a rough voice cry out, "Keep back! This hill belongs to us, and we do not allow anyone to cross it."

"Who are you?" asked the Scarecrow.

Out from the rock stepped the strangest man the travelers had ever seen. He was short and stout. His big head was flat on the top and supported by a thick neck. He had no arms at all.

Because the man had no arms, the Scarecrow could not imagine how he would stop them from climbing the hill. But as soon as the Scarecrow started up, the man's head shot forward and his neck stretched out. The flat top of his head struck the Scarecrow in the middle and sent him tumbling over and over down the hill. A chorus of laughter came from hundreds of other Hammer-Heads, who were hiding behind the rocks.

"Call the Winged Monkeys," the Tin Woodman suggested to Dorothy. She put on the Golden Cap and did so at once.

The monkeys were as prompt as ever. They carried the group over the hill, too high for the angry Hammer-Heads to reach them, and set them down in the country of the Quadlings. Here all the houses were painted red, and everyone had red clothes, for red was the Quadlings' favorite color.

At last, Dorothy and her friends came to a very beautiful castle. Before the gates were three young girls. "Why have you come to the South Country?" one of them asked Dorothy.

"To see the good Witch who rules here," she answered. "Will you take us to her?"

"Of course," said the girls. They led the weary travelers into the castle. They were shown into a room where Glinda the Witch sat upon a throne of rubies.

"What can I do for you, my child?" she asked Dorothy kindly.

Dorothy told the Witch her story. When she'd finished, Glinda leaned forward and kissed her.

"I am sure I can tell you how to get back to Kansas," Glinda said. "But you must give me the Golden Cap. With it I will send the Scarecrow, the Tin Woodman, and the Lion back where they belong."

"Gladly!" Dorothy agreed, and handed the Good Witch the Cap. "But how can I get back to Kansas?"

"Your silver shoes will carry you there," replied Glinda. "If you had known their power, you could have gone home the very first day you came to this country."

"But then I should not have had my wonderful brains!" cried the Scarecrow.

"And I should not have had my lovely heart," said the Tin Woodman.

"And I should have lived a coward forever," said the Lion.

"This is all true," Dorothy said, "and I am glad to have helped you all. But now my fondest wish is to go back to Kansas."

"All you have to do is knock the heels of the shoes together three times and command the shoes to carry you wherever you wish to go," Glinda instructed her.

Dorothy was ready to do just that. But first she had to say farewell to all her new friends. The Tin Woodman started to cry in a way that threatened to rust his joints. Dorothy was crying, too, for it was hard to say good-bye to such wonderful companions.

Finally, Glinda gave Dorothy a kiss, and the little girl was ready to go home. She picked up Toto in her arms. Then she clicked the heels of her shoes together three times, saying, "Take me home to Aunt Em!"

Instantly, Dorothy was whirling through the air so swiftly that all she felt was the wind whistling past her ears. Then she stopped so suddenly that she rolled over on the grass several times before she knew where she was.

Dorothy sat up and looked around her. She was sitting on the broad Kansas prairie. In front of her was the new farmhouse Uncle Henry had built. Toto jumped out of her arms and ran toward the barn, barking joyfully.

Dorothy stood up and saw that she no longer had on her silver shoes. But they were forgotten as soon as she saw Aunt Em coming out of the house.

"My darling child!" Aunt Em cried as Dorothy ran to her. "Where in the world did you come from?"

"From the Land of Oz," Dorothy told her. "And oh, Aunt Em, I'm so glad to be home again!"